Benoni Dickerman

The blood-stained cross, a messianic lyric or the Birth, life, death,

resurrection and ascension of Jesus, the Christ

Benoni Dickerman

The blood-stained cross, a messianic lyric or the Birth, life, death, resurrection and ascension of Jesus, the Christ

ISBN/EAN: 9783743335486

Manufactured in Europe, USA, Canada, Australia, Japa

Cover: Foto ©Andreas Hilbeck / pixelio.de

Manufactured and distributed by brebook publishing software
(www.brebook.com)

Benoni Dickerman

The blood-stained cross, a messianic lyric or the Birth, life, death, resurrection and ascension of Jesus, the Christ

THE
BLOOD-STAINED CROSS;

A MESSIANIC LYRIC,

OR

THE BIRTH, LIFE, DEATH, RESURREC-
TION AND ASCENSION

OF

JESUS, THE CHRIST.

————

BY BENONI DICKERMAN.

————

COLUMBUS, OHIO:
FRED J. HEER, PRINTER.
1884.

PREFACE.

The author of the following lines has not imitated "Cunningly devised fables," but deeply deplores the general hankering for fictitious trash. More accustomed to the use of the axe and plow than to the pen; having passed his three score and ten years, during three score of which he has been connected with various Sabbath Schools; but now by infirmities of age being debarred that chosen employ, he seeks in an unpretentious way to continue to teach

"WHEN I AM GONE."

THE AUTHOR,
CONSTANTIA, O.

Sent by mail on receipt of price, $1.00.

(iii)

INTRODUCTION.

———◆———

The theme of this Lyric is one that has never been exhausted, and never will be, while the hopes of men cluster around the atoning work of Christ. To every Christian mind it presents itself in terms of his own personal experience. So many, and so profound are the mysteries which surround the Messiah, the God-man, that few thoughtful minds are fully satisfied with any forthsetting of others. Every earnest soul wants to set forth more clearly to himself the whole story from the Manger at Bethlehem, to the Ascension from Olivet. Every one that has done this for himself, feels that he has got new light. He feels that what has helped him will help others. And so he feels impelled, not by the craving for authorship, but by the hope of doing good, to give his thought to the world.

Such is obviously the inspiration of this little Book. It lays no claim to artistic merit as Poetry. It aims to set forth in rhyme the Author's conception of the wondrous story of THE BIRTH, LIFE,

(v)

DEATH, RESURRECTION, AND ASCENSION OF JESUS, THE CHRIST. In this form doubtless it will gain the attention of some who would not be attracted by the same thoughts in the form of prose. They will find in it only "the old, old story." But it may set in a new light, and fix upon the memory, scenes in the "Wonderful Life," which no Christian would let slip.

If any apology for its publication is needed, it may be found in the Words of the Dreamer, who set forth his ideal of the Christian life, in the "Pilgrim's Progress."

> "Thus I set pen to paper with delight,
> And quickly had my thoughts in black and white,
> Well, when I had put my ends together,
> I showed them others, to see whether
> They would condemn them, or them justify;
> And some said, Let him live; some, Let him die;
> Some said, John, print it; others said, Not so,
> Some thought it might do good; others said No,
> At last I thought, since you are thus divided,
> I print it will; and so the case decided."

W. E. MOORE, D. D.

COLUMBUS, O.

Contents.

———✦———

MISCELLANEOUS POEMS—*Continued.*

THE BLOOD-STAINED CROSS.

In the Blood-stained Cross I glory—
  Trust its merits, not my own;
Let me sing the wondrous story
  How for sin did Christ atone.

In remotest age eternal,
  Through the ages yet to be,
God alone on Throne supernal
  Comprehends infinity.

Ere the dawning of creation,
  Or the march of time began,
Ere the Sun assumed his station
  Or was made primeval man;

Erst the twinkling stars of heaven
  Lighted up the galaxy,
Or the lightning flash was given
  Gleaming o'er the land and sea;

Darkness reigned—chaotic darkness—
  Through the realms of boundless night;
Then amid the gloomful blackness
  Spoke the Word: "Let there be light!"

Suddenly in boundless measure
  Shone the starry worlds of light;
Sparkling gems and sparkling treasure,
  Lo! the darkness takes its flight.

Who is He that by His power
  Spoke from naught each sparkling gem—
Source of light in darkest hour
  Made them for His diadem?

Who is He that weighs each mountain?
  Poises every ponderous world?
Measures every ocean fountain?
  Sees them in confusion whirled?

I'll rehearse the names He beareth
  Of each name deserving well!
Say what chieftain's name compareth
  With the name Immanuel?

Who appeared in human nature,—
  Might I trace by help Divine
All His works of every feature
  And His form incarnadine.

Wondrous are the names He beareth,
  Names unlike the names of men
Who a bloody vesture weareth
  These employ my lab'ring pen.

How He walks upon the water,
  Stills the tumult of the wave,
Brings to life Ja-i-rus' daughter,
  Rescues Laz'rus from the grave.

Heals the congenital blindness
  Of a man to sorrow born,
By His superhuman kindness;
  Darkness flees before the morn'.

He expels a legion devils
  From one man—a Gadarene—
Gave release from many evils
  By a word, as " Be thou clean !"

I'll record His life of sorrow,
    And the cruel death He died;
I no fiction need to borrow,
    He for man was crucified.

All the pens of seers and sages,
    Half His wonders ne'er have told;
Other pens in future ages
    Still new wonders shall unfold.

Ere the garden was vacated
    In the hour of sorest need—
Adam's fear was then abated
    By the promise of the "Seed!"

Through the mist of future ages
    Abram saw the promised "Seed."
Faith engraved fond mem'rys pages
    Gave him strength in time of need.

Moses told the Hebrew nation
    Of a "Prophet" that should come.
Make for Him due preparation—
    "Eat the lamb" in every home.

Israel taught by strange devices
   Understood alone through faith;
Bloody rites and sacrifices
   Typified His shameful death.

Amoz' son—ordained of Heaven
   Once to see the Seraphim,
Writes "To us a Son is given,"
   Only Son of Elohim.

Other men in other ages
   Wrote of one who should appear;
This we read in sacred pages
   Unmistakable and clear.

"Mighty God," the "lasting Father,"
   "Prince of peace," His names shall be;
He shall all the nations gather
   From the islands of the sea.

"Wonderful" in works of healing,
   "Wonderful" in works of grace,
While His sympathetic feeling
   Far transcends the human race.

"Counselor," fit appellation,
   From His Father He obtains,
"The desire of every nation"
   For He comes to break their chains.

Jacob's "Star" guiding the sages
   To the Babe of Bethlehem,
Seen by prophets through the ages—
   Dimly seen through types of them.

E'en the angels filled with wonder
   Fain would scan obscurity:
Fain would part the veil asunder,
   Penetrate futurity.

Many longing ones are waiting
   Like the aged Simeon,
Hope and fear oft' alternating
   Waiting for the promised One!

Now the Scepter has departed
   And the Oracles are dumb;
Patient be, ye broken-hearted,
   Jacob's "Shiloh" soon will come.

With no pompous demonstration,
    With not sound of fife and drum,
Nor with outward observation
    Shall the promised Savior come.

Daniel, who among their number
    The Messiah did foretell;
Visions saw in nightly slumber,
    Saw the King of Israel.

On the margin of their waters,
    Euphrates and Hiddekel,
Magi met fair Salem's daughters
    In amazement heard them tell

What the Hebrew prophets told them,
    Unto One to bow the knee;
How their many gods had sold them
    Into long captivity.

Amos' son, and Jeremiah,
    Through prophetic insight trace
Pointing to the great Messiah
    To restore the chosen race.

Hark! The mandate comes from Heaven—
  Comes to all the cherubim.
No exemption now is given,
  " All ye angels, worship Him!"

Instantly those angel minions
  Come—like morning rays they come,
Wafted on etherial pinions,
  Where the watchful shepherds roam.

Sure no prophecy can vary
  Of the " Branch" from Jesse's stem.
Joseph and the Virgin Mary
  Must abide at Bethlehem.

Jesse's son in former ages
  Tuned his harp to songs of praise—
Lofty thought his heart engages
  Where he spends his youthful days.

He, the ruddy, tuneful shepherd,
  Guards the flock by night and day;
From the lion, or the leopard,
  Bears the helpless lamb away.

Gabriel comes, thrice welcome angel,
  Joyful news for man to bring.
Shepherds hail the glad evangel
  Tidings of the infant King.

Thus they sing, angelic legions—
  "Glory be to God on high.
Peace and love through all earth's regions,"
  Songs abound and multiply.

Nature smiles, the earth is vernal,
  Sharon's roses clothe the ground,
Cloudless is the sky nocturnal,
  Nature's silence is profound.

From the East with costly treasure,
  Not for show nor vain pretense,
Wise men bring, in princely measure,
  " Myrrh, and gold, and frankincense."

To a bloody rite subjected
  Ere the eighth day had expired;
No command by Him neglected
  Though in swaddling clothes attired.

Ere full forty days were ended
  To the temple He was borne,
Type and antitype were blended
  Like the golden hues of morn.

Simeon, who long had waited,
  There embraced the holy Child,
And of Anna 'tis related
  How with joy her heart was filled.

Now when danger was impending,
  Danger to the blessed Child,
Gabriel, his Ward defending,
  The foul scheme of malice foiled.

While in quiet they were sleeping,
  He the timely warning gave.
Those are safe whom He is keeping,
  Like protection may we have.

Scarce He entered on His mission
  Ere they thirsted for His blood.
How amazing His condition!
  Come, behold the Son of God.

Trembling fugitive, behold Him,
  Fleeing from His native land;
In her arms see Mary fold Him,
  O'er the barren, burning sand.

Short His stay—the infant Stranger
  In the land of Pha-ra-oh,
Who was cradled in a manger
  In the ages long ago.

Soon the fugitives returning
  Cautiously their way retrace,
Heed their guardian angel's warning,
  Nazareth their resting place.

There His childhood days glide gently
  As the silent waters go,
Pensive oft, while He intently
  Contemplates this world of woe.

Yet we find Him in the the temple;
  See the young, precocious Child,
Through His answers, questions ample;
  With amazement all are filled.

While the people are awaiting
  For some mighty conqueror,
Some great chieftain, demonstrating
  His abilities in war;

Lo! a man of humble station,
  Clad in garments coarse and plain,
Startles all the Hebrew nation
  Like a whirlwind o'er the plain.

Malachi foretold His coming;
  Him Elijah, he surnamed:
Through the dim and distant gloaming
  Sees the erring ones reclaimed.

In appearance and in bearing
  He a prophet seemed to be,
With Elijah well comparing
  In His strange austerity.

From the wilderness emerging
  By the Jordan takes His stand,
There the multitudes converging
  Fain comply with His command.

Trumpet like His voice is sounding;
  Wrapt, they list with mighty joy;
Many hearts in hope are bounding—
  Let this theme my pen employ.

There He speaks, the earnest preacher,
  With a stern severity;
Multitudes wait on the Teacher—
  Pattern of austerity.

"Let a highway be provided
  In the desert for our God,"
Who the waters twice divided
  Where our fathers' feet have trod.

"Bring the fruits of true repentance,
  Flee the wrath that is to come,"
They regard each pointed sentence;
  In each heart truth finds a home.

Let the Jordan's limpid waters
  Typify the Spirit's power,
When upon "My sons and daughters"
  I my cleansing Spirit pour.

Jordan's waters, ever flowing,
    Now by John are utilized;
Multitudes, in sorrow bowing,
    By this prophet were baptized.

Soon appears a youthful stranger
    Mingling with the thronging crowd,
"Man of sorrows," Child of danger,
    Who precocious wisdom showed.

Now Messiah and the preacher
    Hold a solemn interview;
John addressed the wondrous Teacher,
    "Fain I'd be baptized by you."

Then rejoined the loving Savior
    To the man of homely dress—
It becometh our behavior
    "To fulfill all righteousness."

When the typic rite was ended,
    And was closed His fervent prayer,
Then the Dove from heaven descended,
    Type and Antitpye met there.

Only John beheld the spirit
  On that Sacred Head descend,
So this record we inherit,
  "Grace and truth" divinely blend.

Hark! A voice proclaims from heaven,
  "This is my beloved One!"
Unto Him all power is given,
  Unto Him my only Son.

He eludes their observation,
  Seeks the desert solitude!
On His pensive meditation,
  Satan does in vain intrude.

In the wilderness He foiled him,
  Foiled him on the Temple's height;
On the mountain's top despoiled him,
  Put him to a hasty flight.

On the mountain Him attending
  Angel guards, each comprehends;
Jacob's ladder now descending,
  Bringing what the Father sends.

Victor from the conflict turning
  To the place Beth-ab-ara;
John,—the Light still brightly burning,
  Sees in Him the "Morning-star."

In a Galilean village
  He displays His power divine,
Nor did, even human tillage,
  Make like that, such luscious wine.

When the people there awaiting
  In expectancy were hushed;
He the water was translating:
  —Water owned its God and blushed!

Not to mad'ning wine transmuted
  He the water in the jar!
Be to Him no act imputed,
  With man's highest good at war.

There He showed His dawning glory,
  Which at first they vaguely see,
Marvels great adorn the story
  Greater things were yet to be.

In the house for prayer appointed,
  With the thronging multitude
He appears; Of God anointed,
  Who all sacrilege eschewed.

While His hand a scourge is holding
  They behold Him in dismay,
See His holy zeal unfolding,
  Terror drives them all away.

Soon the learned Nicodemus,
  Councilor and Pharisee
Questions Him who would redeem us!
  Like a child at mother's knee.

Timidly when day was ended
  And when darkness spread its pall,
He approached all unattended;
  Like a child at father's call.

"Rabbi! All Thy works bear witness
  Thy commission is from heaven,"
Works divine have proper fitness,
  Not to man such power is given.

Death, through sin all men inherit
  All their righteousness is vain:
Needful is the Holy Spirit,
  For they need be born again.

From the City soon returning,
  Multitudes were then baptized,
They this needed lesson learning,
  Purity is symbolized.

Next to Galilee returning,
  Seeks the place of Jacob's well,
Gives a Gentile woman warning,
  Near " *Elohe-Israel.*"

Thither came the Gentile woman
  At the sultry hour of noon
When the dial with its gnomon
  Brings to mind the cooling boon.

He addressed the Gentile stranger,
  Told her of the Living-Fount',
Warned her of her special danger;
  Not to trust Gerizim' Mount.

Told what service God commanded;
  In the spirit, and in truth;
This of *all* is now demanded,
  Of the aged and the youth.

They entreated, and He tarried
  Teaching them of heavenly ways,
To their hearts the truth was carried
  Through the two succeeding days.

Near to Cana there resided
  In the town Capernaum
One whose trusting heart confided
  When he bade the Master come.

One whose youthful son was burning
  With a raging fever then;
From all human aid is turning,
  Trusting not in human ken.

Chuza and his wife Joanna
  Greet with joy their living son,
Shout aloud their glad hosanna,
  How the joyful tidings run!

Jesus saw one helpless creature,
   Invalid for forty years.
Soon His sympathetic nature,
   Gave relief and stayed his tears.

In the Temple Jesus taught them
   All the sleeping dead should rise,
Whose idolatries had brought them
   Only vanity and lies.

Justice full shall be accorded
   At the rising of the just,
And the wicked be rewarded—
   All in vain their sinful trust.

On the Sabbath, in the city
   Favored high, Capernaum,
Many people seeking pity
   To the great Physician come.

Noisy demons, raging fever,
   Disappear at His behest;
Healing virtue like a river
   Saves the lowly and distressed.

E'en the wretched leper, praying
  Cries aloud, " Lord, cleanse Thou me!"
When He speaks there's no delaying—
  Leprosy itself shall flee.

In the public congregation,
  On the holy Sabbath day,
Rulers of the Jewish nation
  Sought to take His life away.

In the Synagogue one mortal
  There amid the multitude,
Waits inside the sacred portal,
  Him the Master interviewed.

Withered, was his hand suspended,
  But when Jesus spoke the word,
Instantly it was extended,
  To completeness now restored.

On the chilly mountain lonely,
  He employs the hours of night,
Prostrate there in prayer only,
  'Till the dawn of morning light.

Twelve apostles He selected,
  From the land of Galilee;
Publicans were not neglected,
  Well instructed they must be.

Model sermon, rich in beauty,
  Was the sermon on the Mount,
Making plain the path of duty;
  Coming from the parent fount.

Model prayer the Teacher gave them,
  Kindly taught them what. to say;
Pray "Our Father"—(would He have them,)
  "Hallowed be Thy Name alway.

Let Thy Kingdom Holy Father,
  Quickly come o'er land and sea,
To Thy fold the nations gather,
  Let them worship only Thee!

Let Thy will, O! Father holy,
  As in Heaven, on Earth be done,
And all people, high and lowly,
  Bow to Thee, Thou holy One.

Give to us, Thou bounteous Giver,
    Day by day our needful food,
Flow Thy mercy like a river,
    Friend and foe alike include.

All our sins do Thou forgive us,
    For like Thee would we forgive;
In no sore temptation leave us,
    Needful grace may we receive.

From the evil one deliver,
    Keep us from his fatal snare,
"Fiery darts" are in his quiver,
    Keep us in Thy constant care."

Blest are they who heed His teaching,
    Through life's brief and tiresome road;
Human wisdom, far o'erreaching,
    Worthy of the Son of God.

In a city one resided,
    With a Roman garrison,
Who a synagogue provided,
    When the people there had none.

One whose servant was afflicted
  By the palsy, near to death;
But his death was interdicted,
  Through his master's matchless faith.

From the bourne of death so lonely
  Brings to life and health again,
By His mighty power only
  One whose Mother lived at Nain.

From a prison dark and cheerless
  To the distant Galilee;
From the Baptist bold and fearless,
  Now in sad perplexity!

Messengers arrive and query,
  "Art Thou He who was to come?"
John was waiting long and weary,
  Filled with doubt, despair and gloom.

"Go and tell to him that sent you
  What you hear and what you see,"
This the answer I present you,
  This shall clear the mystery.

By request He once was dining
　　With a haughty Pharisee;
There at noon-tide was reclining
　　At the table, leisurely.

Soon there came, not by appointment,
　　One, sore-burdened by her guilt,
Brings a box of precious ointment—
　　See her heart in sorrow melt.

Tenderly behind Him bowing,
　　Demonstrates for Him her love,
While her tears profusely flowing
　　Her devotion to Him prove.

Hear His gracious words then spoken,
　　Words that ease her broken heart,
Of his love a fitting token,
　　O! what joy His words impart.

From a boat launched on the waters
　　He addressed a listening crowd,
From the commonest of matters,
　　Rich instruction He bestowed.

Smoothly o'er the waters gliding,
    In a vessel small and frail;
Soon on angry billows riding,
    In a fierce, tempestuous gale;

He, who made the boundless ocean,
    Holds the tempest in His hand;
Stills the turbulent commotion—
    Winds and waves heed His command.

"Peace! Be still, ye raging billows!"
    Billows echo to the wind;
"Peace!" He speaks! a stillness follows—
    "Hear ye deaf, and look ye blind."

Now the tranquil waters leaving,
    Walking on the eastern shore,
From the tombs adjacent, raving,
    Naked, haggard, fierce and sore,

Comes a man; no fetters bind him,
    Demons hold supreme control;
Jesus speaks, when lo! they mind Him,
    Disenthralled the captive soul.

See Jairus' only daughter,
    Silent in the sleep of death—
He, who walks upon the water,
    Compensates her parents' faith;

Takes by hand the youthful sleeper
    And commands her to arise;
Angel guard has been her keeper,
    Now from death she opes her eyes.

One in poverty was pining,
    Invalid for many years;
Stealthily she touched the lining
    Of the garment that He wears.

Instantly she felt the merit
    Of the Master's healing power,
Both in body and in spirit:
    Blooms in health like morning flower.

Constant were His works of healing,
    Giving vision to the blind;
To His mighty works appealing—
    Proof like this we nowhere find.

Now, His messengers, is sending—
  Does authority impart,
Tells what dangers are impending,
  Springing from satanic art.

Iterates specific labors—
  Urgent is the work to do;
No delay, with friends and neighbors,
  I the pattern set for you.

Like to sheep 'mongst wolves I send you,
  Harmless be like timid dove;
Constantly I will attend you,
  You my faithfulness shall prove.

Give the loathsome leper healing,
  Fiercest demons exorcise,
Give relief to all appealing,
  Bid the sleeping dead arise.

In the desert congregated
  Were five thousand hungry men:
Could their appetite be sated
  In the desert, there and then?

On the grass in ranks reclining,
  He commanded them to be;
After thanks, they all were dining,
  That promiscuous company.

Few the fishes, scant their measure,
  Small the loaves—one-fourth a score;
Could they look with any pleasure
  Were the loaves a hundred more?

From the elements surrounding
  He evolves the needed food,
Thus His enemies confounding
  By the miracles He showed.

When He walks the leaping billow,
  Quick subsides th' obsequious wind;
Like the summer evening mellow
  Now becomes the troubled mind.

With incessant labor weary
  He departs from Galilee;
O'er the dusty way and dreary,
  To the borders of the sea.

There a Gentile woman met Him,
Overwhelmed, sadly distressed,
   Tearfully she did entreat Him,
For her daughter, sore oppressed.

Heed He gave to her petition,
   What she craved He did impart;
Gentile, tho', no inhibition,
   When she came with trusting heart.

Not a stinted crumb, this winner,
   From the Master did receive;
Welcomes He, each trembling sinner,
   If they only do believe.

From a cavern in the mountain
   Thence the Jordan's waters flow,
Gushing from the parent fountain,
   Rushing through the vale below—

So the waters of salvation,
   'From the living Fountain flow,
For the cleansing of the nation,
   Antidote for all our woe!

Peter told Him what men called Him,
  Who the leaping billows trod;
Ere the Master had installed him
  He confessed the Christ of God.

"Here my kingdom I am building,
  Moral architects are ye;
Righteousness its gates is gilding,
  And my *Gospel* is the *key*."

Faith in me is *Rock* foundation,
  Firm and steadfast it shall prove;
No satanic combination,
  Ever shall my Church remove.

Not on Peter, fickle Peter,
  Is the living structure built,
But a better name and sweeter,
  He sustains—who bore our guilt.

When shall fall this granite mountain,
  Tow'ring high—eight thousand feet—
When is dry the ocean fountain,
  May His church sustain defeat.

On Mount Hermon He ascended,
　　Simon Peter, James and John,
Others, two, from heaven descended,
　　What a theme to dwell upon!

Moses to a Mount ascended
　　From the sultry plain below;
There by Joshua attended,
　　On the lofty Mt. Nebo.

Thence surveyed the distant mountains,
　　Carmel, Hermon, Lebanon;
Limpid brooks from crystal fountains;
　　But his work on earth was done!

There he died the faithful Moses,
　　At the age thrice forty years,
Michael guards where he reposes;
　　Not there Satan interferes.

There Jehovah had provided,
　　Just for him a lonely grave;
In Jehovah he confided;
　　Nothing more for him to crave.

There no costly shaft arises
   Like man makes for earl or duke,
Better for what God devises—
   Moses left the *Pentateuch!*

There was one distinguished seer,
   And a holy Man of God,
Not on earth had he a peer,
   Yet in solitude abode.

On Mt. Carmel Ahab met him,
   Ahab with four hundred men;
There they craftily beset him
   Instigated by the Queen.

There the fire from heaven descended,
   And consumed the sacrifice;
From all harm is he defended,
   While to God on high he cries.

He from threatened danger fleeing,
   Makes a tiresome pilgrimage;
Weary of his earthly being,
   Finds a welcome beverage.

3

Then the fugitive and stranger
  Skims along where Moses walked;
Lo! The way-worn desert ranger,
  Talks with God as Moses talked!

Hush! The solid rocks are rending
  By the earthquake, and the wind;
But Jehovah's voice befriending
  Calms the frightened prophet's mind.

Not at Horeb may he tarry,
  But must hasten on his way:
He has messages to carry
  Which admit of no delay.

Something better was provided,
  For his servant by the Lord,
Who by man was here derided;
  Nought like it could earth afford,

By his mantle he divided
  Waters which from Hermon flow,
There a chariot was provided
  Just across from Jericho.

See him rising, rising, rising;
  Fifty prophets see him rise;
Wonderful! O! How surprising;
  Through the blue etherial skies.

On Mount Hermon, heavenward rising
  Prophets two, apostles three—
(I no fiction am devising—)
  These comprise the company.

O! The glory, bright, transcendent;
  Beaming from his form Divine;
With strange visitants attendant,
  See his face the sun outshine.

Beaming from within this glory,
  Beaming through this fleshly veil;
Wonderful this strange, strange story,
  Satan could not countervail.

The Shekinah was apparent,
  As of Old it did appear,
Which Almighty power did warrant,
  While Elohim's voice they hear.

Matthew tells how Simon Peter,
　　As directed by the Lord;
Takes a fish and finds a *Stater*,
　　Just according to his word.

Strange deposit, safe awaiting
　　His behest, whom brutes obey;
No event His plans frustrating,
　　Nor His purposes can stay.

Hear! He calls the thirsty to Him,
　　"If you thirst come unto me;"
Living water flowing through Him
　　Now is offered full and free.

Light effulgent now is streaming
　　To illume the moral world;
Lo! "The Morning Star" is gleaming,
　　Darkness from its seat is hurled.

While the angry Jews beset Him
　　He asserts His rightful claim;
Yet they scornfully entreat Him
　　And condemn the *Great-I-am*.

At Mt. Olivet resided
    Just a little family;
For His wants they well provided
    At their home in Bethany,

On His journey, weary often,
    Sought He rest at close of day;
Mutual love can labor soften,
    Sympathy can care allay,

Martha and her sister Mary,
    Lazarus, all tried and true,
Oft refreshing Him when weary,
    Gentle as the evening dew.

At Beth-abara He tarried,
    On the Jordon's eastern shore;
One a message to Him carried
    Of affliction, sudden, sore.

Ere He reached the place of weeping
    On the Jordon's western side
Lazarus who seemed but sleeping,
    In reality had died.

In a gloomy cave they place him,
　　Roll a stone against the door;
Shall they never more embrace him?
　　Count the days, one, two, three, four.

At the proper time, the Master
　　Comes again to Bethany;
Now, O! Death! Thou ruthless waster,
　　He shall set thy captive free.

"Jesus wept" with weeping Mary,
　　Bade them take the stone away;
Scarcely longer could He tarry;
　　For a moment hear Him pray.

"Lazarus!" the Master speaketh,
　　He has loosed Death's iron band,
And His voice the silence breaketh,
　　Death itself heeds His command.

Soon ten outcast lepers met Him,
　　As He wends His weary way;
Nor in vain do they entreat Him,
　　For He takes their plague away.

Going on toward the city,
  Where so many prophets died,
While His heart o'erflows in pity,
  Takes His friends—the twelve aside.

Tells them what was Him awaiting,
  At the coming Paschal feast,
Carefully, the things relating
  To His foes, the scribe and priest.

Tells them of the cup baptismal,
  He and they must be baptized;
Brief the conflict, dreadful, dismal,
  When He should be sacrificed.

When they'd passed the ancient city;
  Which the wary spies did view,
One solicited His pity,
  Ere He reached the city new.

Jesus there relieved his blindness,
  Who was called Bartimeus,
Still His heart is filled with kindness,
  He will do the same for us.

While in Simon's house a resting,
  Mary, Martha, Lazarus;
Mary, well her Love attesting,
  Good example, sets for us.

Pours the costly precious ointment,
  On her Masters sacred head:
Not by chance, 'twas Heaven's appointment,
  Christ commends the worthy deed.

Martha served at Simon's table,
  Lazarus was Simon's guest,
Love unites them like a cable.
  Most divinely they are blest!

By the wayside, quite apparent,
  See a barren, fig-tree stand;
Then for fruit it gave no warrant,
  "Fruitless be" is His command.

Nought but leaves it had afforded,
  Withered soon they all shall be;
On the morrow was recorded
  "Withered leaves; sterility."

They their garments cast before Him,
  With palm branches strew the ground.
With Hosannas they adore Him,
  Hill and dale reflect the sound.

Zion's King is riding slowly,
  On a beast unused before;
David's Son is meek and lowly,
  Crowds assemble more and more.

Instantly all sing " Hosanna,"
  Like the bursting of a flame;
Rocks and hills resound " Hosanna,"
  Children join the loud acclaim.

Trickling tear-drops chase each other,
  Wearing channels down His cheek;
"Man of sorrows," "Elder Brother."
  Half Thy sorrows who can speak?

He foretold the desolation,
  Which He saw was soon to be,
Of their city, and their nation,—
  With prophetic certainty.

Now again within the Temple
　　He rebukes their greed for gain,
By remonstrance, stern and ample,
　　He expelled them thence again.

Now at length He leaves the Temple,
　　Never more will He return;
Ne'er was seen such sad example,
　　In compassion see Him yearn.

From this hour "My Father save me,"
　　"Father glorify Thy name!"
In this sorrow do not leave me
　　For, to rescue man I came.

Hark! From heaven a voice resounding,
　　Coming through the vaulted sky,—
Twice before that voice was sounding—
　　"I my name will glorify."

Privately, on Olive seated,
　　He the future brings to view,
Tells them of His work completed,
　　In this dispensation new.

He foreshows the Roman legions,
  And the Temple's overthrow;
Omens in the upper regions,
  Darkness o'er the land below.

Dark the evening; sad the greeting,
  In the place for Him prepared.
With His twelve disciples meeting
  Every heart profoundly stirred.

He performed a servant's duty;
  For He washed their sev'ral feet;
Pattern set of graceful beauty
  And humility complete.

Most surprising was that warning,
  "One of you shall me betray,"
E're the coming of the morning
  All of you will flee away.

Then He used as sacred emblem
  Simply bread, and simply wine,
After thanks, He gave unto them,—
  Soon He would His life resign.

Bread and wine revive the fainting;
　So His body and His blood,
When the heart for God is panting,
　Constitute substantial food.

"Eat this bread, 'tis fitting token,
　Drink this cup it shows my death,"
Keep in mind the words I've spoken,
　In my Gospel rest your faith.

Gathered at that final meeting,
　Seated round the Paschal board;
They the typic lamb were eating,—
　The disciples and their Lord.

The prescient Master told them,
　One of them would Him betray;
One of them would thrice deny Him;
　All of them would run away.

Treach'rous Judas quickly leaving,
　Hastes His crafty foes to meet;
To preclude any deceiving,
　Bids them seize whom he should greet.

Valiant Peter, self-reliant,
  With his hand upon his sword—
Proud bravado! How defiant!—
  Ne'er would he forsake his Lord!
    .

Eagerly to Him they listen,
  Listen till the midnight hour;
All inquietude they chasten.
  Grasp His words of silent power.

Lest they loose them, He assures them,
  Of the coming Paraclete;
Its fulfillment well secures them,
  Makes their memory complete.
    .

Having crossed the Cedron valley,
  Soon they reach Mount Olivet;
To forget were worse than folly;
  Tears could ne'er repay the debt.

Tongue of angel, might I borrow
  To portray the heavy load;
Ne'er on earth was seen such sorrow
  As o'erwhelmed the Son of God.

Ne'er shall fail one jot or tittle,
  Of the things of Him foretold;—
Though to man it seem but little—
  One by one, shall all unfold.

Having reached the place appointed,
  He selects the favored three,
They attend Him, God's Anointed,
  There in sad Gethsemane.

For a little space He leaves them,
  Yet bespeaks their sympathy;
His stupendous sorrow grieves them,
  In the dark Gethsemane.

Prone upon the earth He's falling,
  In the garden's shady bower;
Hear Him cry—O! How appalling—
  "Father save me from this hour!"

See! The bloody sweat is rushing
  From His face, a crimson tide,
Forced by agony so crushing;
  "Why Thy face my Father hide?"

But the three are lost in slumber;
    He the wine-press treads alone;
None among the chosen number,
    But whose friendship seems withdrawn.

"Father! Take this cup of sorrow"
    Now from me, Thine only Son,
Lest I fall by Death's fell arrow,
    Ere my chosen work be done.

But the bitter, dreadful chalice
    He must drain, nor would decline,
Though His foes, from hellish malice,
    Jew and Gentile, all combine.

While He struggles there in anguish,
    Gabriel comes with skill Divine;—
There no longer may He languish—
    Brings from heaven an anodyne.

Now from sleep, the three awaking,
    Asks them, "Would ye rest and sleep?"
Me your Master now forsaking?
    Well might Salem's daughters weep.

Hark! What mean those foot-steps stealing,
  Stealthily as bandits steal?
Torch and lantern, now revealing
  Fiends, that make the blood congeal.

Vain, their war-like preparation,
  Their munitions all in vain;
He who came for man's salvation,
  Was from earth's foundation slain.

When He saw the band approaching
  With their clubs, their swords and spears,
On that hallowed place encroaching,
  In His mien, no fear appears.

He advances then to meet them,
  Fearing not the fierce array;
Kindly, gently, would He greet them,—
  Who but Judas leads the way?

With great blandishment he hailed Him,
  And he kissed Him, to excess;
But the Master thus unveiled him
  "Thou betray'st me with a kiss!"

Soldiers turn their backs toward Him,
  On the ground they headlong fall;—
(He'd no friends at hand to guard Him—)
  "Conscience made them cowards all."

When they rally, then they bind Him,
  Safely with a leathern thong;
Crowds before Him, crowds behind Him,
  He's a lamb, to slaughter borne.

Well was Peter's courage tested,
  Valiantly he wields his sword;
When the Master was arrested
  By the midnight surging horde.

There his well poised falchion gleaming
  Cleaves the luckless Malchus' ear.
He a dashing hero seeming,
  But his rashness cost him dear.

Then the Master chided Peter,
  Healed the wound his sword had made,
Meekly bore the irksome fetter,—
  Peter sheathed his gory blade.

4

Peter follows near the rabble
  In the path the Master trod.
Listens to the jeering babble,
  As they mock the Son of God.

Simon must like wheat be sifted,
  And the chaff must be consumed;
With true courage was he gifted,
  But he needs to be illumed.

Soon they reach Caiaphas' palace
  In the darkness of the night;
Thirst for blood, and fiendish malice
  Scarce can wait the morning light.

There he saw Caiaphas' waiter,
  In great hurry, passing near;
Fix his flashing eye on Peter;
  Whisper in the portress' ear.

Thus environed in the palace,
  Hope departed, courage fled;
Peter cower'd before their malice
  When confronted by the maid.

Much bewildered then was Peter,.
    There inveigled by the crowd;
For the moment it seemed better
    To abjure: he disavow'd

All connection with the Master,
    Jesus Christ, of Galilee;
Then his fears came fast, and faster,
    Like the wavelets of the sea.

There by Satan was he sifted,
    But the chaff was blown away;
Soon the sombre cloud was lifted
    And his faith resumed the sway.

O! That kindly look of Jesus,
    Melts his heart in contrite tears.
It from bitter sorrow frees *us*,
    Dissipates *our* doubts and fears.

Yet the Master, still forsaken,
    Treads the wine-press all alone.
But the work He's undertaken
    Very soon will all be done.

See the people vainly raging,
　　Futile all that they devise;
War against Jehovah waging,
　　They fulfill the prophecies.

Quickly was His doom decided
　　By the Jews and Roman power
All, by fiendish malice guided,
　　In that dark, and dreadful hour.

While the multitude were sleeping
　　Quietly all through the night,
Frenzied men in ward, were keeping
　　Him, the victim of their spite.

He the galling fetter bearing,
　　In the Council is arraigned,
Annas then the Ephod wearing
　　That prerogative maintained.

Pertinent the answers given,
　　To the questions, meant a snare;
When that cruel blow was driven,
　　Meekness showed beyond compare.

To Caiaphas, Annas sent Him,
  Like a lamb to slaughter brought;
They through fraud would circumvent Him.
  Every charge with falsehood fraught.

Patiently He looks and listens,
  Yet He opens not his mouth;
Truth confessed, His death but hastens
  Even in the prime of youth.

"I adjure thee, I adjure thee,"
  Said Caiaphas unto Him;
Let no flitting hope allure thee,
  Thou the Son of Elohim?

"Yes I am," The truth is spoken,
  And all power to me is given,
I to you will show my token,
  Coming in the clouds of heaven.

Now they rave and madly spite Him,
  Blinding now His weeping eyes;
Jeer, and spit, they push and smite Him—
  More than this can hell devise?

Yes, with cruel blows repeated,
  They enjoin Him " Prophesy "
Your imposture is defeated,
  Your pretensions we defy.

Him they bring to Pontius Pilate,
  Bring in chains to Pilate's bar;
As men chain the blood-stained pirate
  Captive in relentless war.

Few the questions then propounded,
  Brief the answers Jesus gave;
Thus the Roman is confounded,
  By the Captive, silent, grave.

Pilate tells the Jews assembled—
  Every charge was false pretense;
All their witnesses dissembled,
  " I maintain His innocense."

Even Herod's cunning failed him,
  Nor elicited a word;
For " That fox " found nought avail'd him,
  Save two men were in accord.

Fain would Pilate rescue Jesus,
  Gladly set the Captive free;
Give discharge to Him who frees us
  From our own captivity.

But he finds Himself unable
  To dissuade the angry crowd;
Priest and ruler join the rabble,
  With one voice they cry aloud.

"Whom shall I release unto you?"
  Was the question put to them;
Take your choice, this moment do you,
  I ,no act of His condemn.

They elect a conspirator,
  One whose hands were stained with blood,
To the race of Man a traitor,
  And reject the Son of God!

"What shall I then do with Jesus?
  Say, what evil hath he done?"
What calamity may seize us,
  If we end what we've begun?

"Crucify Him!" "Crùcify Him!"
  Is the loud incessant cry;
"Crucify Him!" We defy Him!
  Nothing less than crucify.

"Hush! They add this imprecation
  On ourselves and children too,
Be His blood." Ah sinful nation!
  What is done, you can't undo.

How they scourge the Man of Sorrows,
  Who our ransom fully paid;
Plough His quiv'ring flesh in furrows,
  Crown with thorns His sacred head.

In a gaudy robe regale Him,
  Mock the scepters monarchs use;
Bow the knee and loudly hail Him,
  Mocking: "Hail, King of the Jews!"

Soon the final preparation
  For His tragic death is made;
The "Desire of every nation."
  Bears the Cross they on Him laid.

Soon He sinks beneath the burden,
　Weak from fasting, loss of blood;
They enforce this cruel guerdon
　On the spotless Lamb of God.

Simon bears the cross before Him,
　Followed by a weeping crowd;
They bewail Him, they deplore Him,—
　See their heads in sorrow bowed.

Jesus turned and looked upon them
　With profoundest sympathy;
Tenderly did He enjoin them
　In these words—"Weep not for Me!"

Tells them what was them awaiting,
　Tells them of their City's doom;
Providence their schemes frustrating,
　Whelming them in live-long gloom.

They denude the fainting Jesus,
　Nail His hands, and nail His feet,
To "The Blood-Stained Cross" that frees us,
　Makes us for His kingdom meet.

Then a wine-cup was presented,
   Not like that in Cana made;
To no opiate He consented,
   Looked to God for present aid.

Gentile soldiers, most unfeeling,
   .Pierce His hands, and ankles too;
Thus to God is He appealing,
   "For they know not what they do."

Others, two were placed beside Him,
   On His right, and on His left,
'Twas not strange that they deride Him,
   Hardened by repeated theft.

Then a title was suspended,
   From the Cross above His head,
But the Jews were much offended
   Who that superscription read.

On a tablet was appearing
   What the angry priests confuse,
Blazoned fair; this title bearing,
   "Jesus is King of the Jews."

Frantic men their malice venting
  Wag the head and bow the knee;
Priest and ruler, all combining
  Join the gen'ral mockery.

E'en the callous malefactor,
  On the right, and on the left
Each in railing was an actor,
  Of humanity bereft.

But the one at last relented,
  In his dire extremity,
Lo! In this we see presented,
  Marvel of sublimity;

While in tears, his eyes are streaming,
  He is filled with glad surprise,
Light Divine on darkness gleaming,
  Now at hand is Paradise.

Near the "Blood-Stained Cross" was Mary,
  So was John, whom Jesus loved;
Jesus, though so worn and weary;
  Was by tender pity moved.

He to John entrusted Mary,
  Filial was His last command;
Friends desert, when fortunes vary
  Duties still must know no end.

Now 't is noon, yet darkness dismal
  Palls the land, like primeval night,
While the darkness so abyssmal
  Veiled the Son of God from sight.

" Eli, lama sabachthani ? "
  Hear the dying Savior cry,
Tell me Father, is there any
  Succor for me, ere I die?

Grief the Savior's heart has broken,
  No such sorrow earth had seen,
Other words must yet be spoken,
  These shall end the dreadful scene.

Great the work of God's Anointed,
  "It is finished!"—finished well!
Finished all that God appointed,
  Finished by Immanuel.

"To Thy hand I yield my spirit."
  Father, I return to Thee;
All in Heaven with joy may hear it,
  Joy be lost in ecstacy.

Now the grief-worn Man of sorrows
  Bows in death His sacred head;
Dried those tears, that ran in furrows;
  He is numbered with the dead.

Terribly the earth is shaking,
  And the Veil is rent in twain;
Why! Is God the earth forsaking?
  Nature groans as if in pain.

There His body still remaining,
  With a spear they pierce His side—
(Prophecy, the deed constraining—)
  Ope' afresh the cleansing tide.

One prophetic declaration
  Yet remained to be fulfilled;
There was made an excavation,
  In a garden Joseph tilled.

There did Joseph bear in sorrow,
　Tenderly, his Savior dead;
That new Tomb did Jesus borrow,
　"He'd not where to lay His head."

Nicodemus, from his treasure
　Brings fine linen, clean and white;
Spices brings in lib'ral measure
　Ere the coming of the night,

They enwrap, and placing surely,
　In a rocky vault alone,
Him they love; and place securely
　At the door, a pond'rous stone,

Warden angel kept the portal,
　Where the Lord of angels lay;
Rest in peace, Thou King Immortal,
　Till the great Sabbatic day.—

Into Hades He descended,
　"To the nether Paradise."
By no escort was attended,
　On a doubtful enterprise.

There the "spirits in that prison,"
  Who foretold His coming, there
Waited till their Savior risen,
  Should the prison gates unbar.

There had angels borne the beggar
  Dying at the rich man's gate;
O'er the gulf, the rich man eager,
  Did for cooling water wait.

There were those who mocked at Noah
  Who foretold the coming flood;
'Till Jehovah shut the door.
  And submerged the multitude.—

Soldiers came, with falchions gleaming
  Carefully they seal the stone;
Of no danger are they dreaming
  'Till two days and nights are gone.

"Not in Hades wilt Thou leave me,
  Nor my flesh corruption see,"
"Not like man wilt Thou deceive me,
  Ope' the gate and set me free!"

While the Roman Guard is sleeping,
  Lo! An angel clothed in white;
Strange authority receiving;
  Comes on wings of morning light.

What cares he for Pontius Pilate,
  Minion of Imperial Rome?
What to him is Cæsar's mandate
  And his seal upon the tomb?

What cared he 'though all earth's legions
  Guard the place where Jesus lay?
Brightness from the upper regions
  Soon should fill them with dismay.

Gabriel comes to ope' the portal,
  Rolling thence the stone away;
Wake's to life the King Immortal
  On the new Sabbatic day.

Death was vanquished by the Sleeper,
  On the morning of that day,
Gabriel joins the inside keeper—
  Very short will be their stay.

Roman Soldiers, frightened badly,
  To the City run away;
Forge a lie, for money gladly;
  No one did that fraud betray.

At the dawning of the morning
  Timid women come in haste,
Nor had they a prior warning,
  Like the Magi from the East.

Now with throbbing hearts they hasten
  To the place where Jesus lay;
Flowing tears, like dew-drops glisten,
  "Who will roll the stone away?"

Friend or foe, they know not whether,
  Had unbarred the entrance door;
Hope and fear, perplexing pother,
  Fear prevailing more and more.

Mary runs back to the City
  Bearing most unwelcome word;
Those who heard were filled with pity—
  They have borne away my Lord.

Some remained when she departed,
  Lab'ring still, in doubt and fear,
While the world was merry hearted,
  He was gone, they held most dear.

Soon with falt'ring step and slowly,
  Enter they the Sepulcher;
Whom they sought, so pure and holy,
  Was no longer lying there.

There two white robed angels tarried,
  Leisurely where He had lain;
While sad tidings Mary carried,
  Having sought her Lord in vain.

Highly honored legates royal,
  Who the tidings break to them;
Highly honored women loyal,
  First to hear the joyful theme.

Fear ye not ye broken-hearted,
  Neither be ye terrified;
He has risen, the tomb deserted,
  Seek not here the Crucified.

They return in great commotion,
   And obtain tho' wan and pale;
Recompense, for their devotion,
   Jesus calls to them " All hail!"

Two disciples soon appearing,
   Peter and the youthful John;
Some intrigue still vaguely fearing,
   Were convinced the Lord was gone.

When they saw not there the Master,
   But the clothes in order laid;
Thought came rushing faster, faster,
   He had risen from the dead.

Mary follows John and Peter,
   To the place of sepulture;
Coming there a little later,
   Looks inside the open door.

Angels speak to weeping Mary
   When they saw her gushing tears,
Should you weep? they kindly query,
   Send away your boding fears.

Mary turned and saw a Stranger,
　　So she thought, but 'twas the Lord.
He had waked, as in the manger
　　Then "Rabboni" she adored.

Two disciples filled with sadness
　　Wend alone the weary way :
But their grief was turned to gladness
　　On that most eventful day.

While they talked of hope frustrated,
　　One, a Stranger, meets with them,
They to Him, at length related
　　What befell Jerusalem.

Told Him all the wondrous story
　　Of the Christ, the Nazarene,—
" Ichabod, departed glory—"
　　And that, angels some had seen.

He the Scriptures then expounded
　　Which foretold His cruel death,
Skeptic hearts thereby confounded;
　　Doubts gave place to joyous faith.

Friendly night had spread its mantle
  O'er the place where they resort,
Then His voice benignant, gentle,
  Quells their fears, who there consort.

"Peace to you" be not affrighted,
  Not like man to you I give;
Scrutiny He then invited,
  "Flesh and blood ye see me have."

Yet once more the Master meets them
  When the Sabbath eve had come;
As before, again He greets them
  In that consecrated room.

"Faithless Thomas reach thy finger,
  Thrust thy hand into my side"—
Let thy doubts no longer linger—
  Which the spear has opened wide.

Thomas saw the wounds remaining,
  Whence the healing current flowed;
Sight of these his faith constraining,
  He exclaims, "My Lord and God!"

To their former craft returning,
  Fishermen of Galilee,
Duties path not yet discerning,
  Launch their boat upon the sea.

Often while the night was waning,
  Cast their net with ill success;
From their labor nothing gaining
  Save the gain of weariness.

When in glory broke the morrow,
  "And the shadows fled away,"
They forgot their toil and sorrow;
  For they heard the Master say

Ye shall find, one effort making,
  "Cast the net on your right hand;"
They comply and soon were taking
  Many fishes to the land.

Three times fifty was the number,
  That the net did there enclose;
Frail the strands which they encumber,
  Yet those strands did not unloose.

He was seen by many others,
　　Half a thousand at one place;
But His love, our Elder Brother's
　　Did the Gentile world embrace.

Thrice He questioned Simon Peter,
　　If he did his Master love;
"Feed my lambs," this proof is better,
　　Love to me this test shall prove.

At Jerusalem they gather
　　To receive His great command,
Soon He's going to His Father,
　　In a better, distant land.

Where so oft' in sorrow meeting,
　　In that sacred upper room;
Kindred spirits hold sad greeting
　　When the final hour had come.

Soon they leave with foot-steps gentle,
　　Hidden from the public view,
Sable night had spread its mantle,
　　Ere they said to Him Adieu!

Having reached their destination
  Favored Mountain, Olivet,
Destined from the world's foundation,
  Man's redemption to complete;

With His pierced hands extended,
  Once again for them He prays;
In a cloud to Heaven ascended:
  Son of God. "Ancient-of-days!"

Many saints in Death's dominions,
  Captive in those dark domains,
Wake, as if on royal pinions,
  Angels came to loose their chains.

Hear their cheerful dulcet voices,
  While the ransomed captives sing—
How the vaulted heaven rejoices,—
  "Where O! Death is now thy sting?"

Swift as thought through starry regions
  Their Redeemer leads the way;
Soon to join Angelic legions,
  In the realms of endless day.

See! The central Orb they're nearing,
  Where *Jehovah* holds His *Throne*,
Where the angels, white robes, wearing,
  Wait for Him who did atone.

At the pearly gates were waiting,
  Looking at the ransomed throng,
There with ardor unabating.
  List to their exultant song.

"Open wide, ye doors supernal,
  Ye debar but death and sin;
And ye pearly gates, eternal;
  Let the King of Glory in!"

"Who is He! This King of Glory?
  Leading this triumphant throng,
Why His garments stained and gory?
  What the meaning of their song?"

Jesus is the King of Glory,
  He is now the Conqueror,
And His garments stained and gory,
  Badges of successful war!

Thus they sing with cheerful voices
  "He redeemed us by His Blood,"
In the Cross each heart rejoices,
  They are kings and priests to God.

Open stand the doors supernal
  Which debar but death and sin,
Since the pearly gates eternal,
  Let the King of Glory in!

THE RETURN.

Word was left when He ascended
  With the ransomed in His train
With the same who Him attended
  He would come to earth again.

'Till Thou come, incarnate Jesus
  We will labor, watch and pray.
Trust that promise, 'till it frees us;
  Why so long is Thy delay?—

In the world's primeval morning
  Man, expelled from Paradise;
To idolatry soon turning,
  Gloated in his shame and vice.

Firm remained the primal seer
  Faithful 'mong the faithless found,
Faithful was, year after year
  'Till three hundred rolled around.

"Enoch walked with God, Jehovah,
    Who foretold him what should be,
Drew aside the misty cover
    Of remote futurity.

He from Adam had descended.
    Generations passed away.
But His servant God befriended
' And the future did portray.

Told him every tribe and nation
    On the earth should be destroyed,
Universal desolation
    Through the agency employed,

By a flood of mighty waters
    Through the supervening days
All of Adam's sons and daughters
    Vengeance meet in dire amaze.

Yet a few, just eight in number
    Should survive the deluge vast;
Undisturbed their quiet slumber
    'Till the indignation passed.

Told to Him the wond'rous story
  Of His Son for sinners slain:
Of His cross, encrimsoned, gory;
  His descent to earth again.

Enoch saw the Judge descending,
  (No injustice did impute;)
With ten thonsand saints attending
  Judgment just to execute.

Through unerring inspiration
  Saw them meet their due rewards;
Rich and poor, of every station
  For their impious deeds and words.

Uniform the sacred teaching
  Touching His return to earth,
To the distant future reaching,
  Planned before Creation's birth.

Angels sang redemption's story
  When they saw the work complete.
Yet again in realms of glory
  Shall the hallowed song repeat.

They attended Him ascending
   To His throne, exalted high;
They will come with Him descending
   And will shout, "The Bridegroom nigh."

When He comes to judge the nations
   He Himself will lead the way,
And assign to all their stations,
   Fill His foes with dire dismay.

Through the long succeeding ages
   Since the Lord ascended high;
Many hearts one thought engages,
   While they wipe the tearful eye.

Hope deferred makes heartfelt sickness,
   Such is human nature here;
For man's strength at best is weakness
   When beset by doubt and fear.

Long the Church for Him has waited,
   Borne the scoffs of wicked men,
Who the Cross of Christ have hated,
   Questioned if He'd come again.

Through succeeding ages waited,
  Careful scanned the prophecies;
He will come, found often stated;
  Trusted in the promises.

Not as at its primal coming
  Will He come the second time;
Now we see the dusky gloaming,
  But we wait time's funeral chime.

When the reaper angels gather
  Harvest of the land and sea;
Then O! holy, righteous Father!
  What shall then the harvest be?

When the Son comes in His glory,
  Saints and angels in His train,
With His vesture stained and gory
  Once the Lamb for sinners slain;

He shall sit on throne supernal,
  And all nations gathered there
Then shall see the King eternal,
  Joyful some, some in despair.—

While the world unconscious sleeping
  Waited for returning day,
Wakeful shepherds vigils keeping
  Hasted where the Savior lay.

Night its sable mantle spreading
  Wrapped the world in calm repose:
When death's captives He was leading
  Rescued from the last of foes.

Yet once more at midnight coming
  As a bridegroom for his bride;
Far beyond the distant gloaming
  Open stands the portal wide.

At the midnight hour—surprising—
  From the summons none can save;
Suddenly the dead are rising
  From the long forgotten grave.

Some for refuge loudly calling,
  None give heed to their demand:
In this day of wrath appalling
  Who shall now have power to stand?

List! A joyful proclamation.
"Come my people to my rest.
Hide with me; this indignation
  Shall at length be overpast."

Now the ambient heavens are burning;
  Earth volcanic feels the woe:
Men for safety vainly yearning;
  Nature feels her mortal throe.

Now appears the Son anointed,
  Throned upon the Judgment seat,
By His Father once appointed
  To fulfil and make complete

All the prophecies betoken;
  Spoke by holy men of old.
For His Word cannot be broken;
  All its links together hold.

Not jot, nor yet one tittle
  Of the word of prophecy
Now shall be accounted little,
  From the first, to Malachi.—

Now upon His throne of glory:
   Near the throne all nations stand;
Greece and Rome, Chaldea hoary;
   Every tribe, from every land;

And await their final sentence
   From the Jews' rejected King.
Nought avails their mock repentance,
   No apology they bring.

Like to goats from sheep divided
   Those to left and these to right;
Righteously has He decided,
   Those to darkness, these to light.

Of His work the consummation
   Is forever now complete:
Earth has passed its conflagration:
   Every foe beneath His feet.

All He undertook is finished,
   Now has come the final end:
From His work was naught diminished,
   God alone could comprehend.

Now the trio, Judas, Pilate
　　And Caiaphas stand aghast;
Stained by blood, like blood-stained pirate
　　And recall the dreadful past.

But the sons of light are carried
　　To their home of light and bliss.
For the Bridegroom, long they tarried,
　　For the Son of Righteousness.

When the trump of Gabriel sounded
　　Heard through heaven, through earth and hell,
Time, so limited and bounded,
　　'Twas of it the funeral knell.

But Eternity! Astounding!
　　Boundless as unmeasured space
Rolls in cycles; thought confounding;
　　Infinite, and measureless.

Not unlike the darkness ancient
　　Is the final darkness now,
Bating this, the old was transient,
　　But this night no morn shall know.

Slow the pendulum is swinging,
  Cycles come and go, between:
Yet no change are eons bringing,
  Though long ages intervene.

MESSIANIC HYMN.

O! Thou who wast ordained of God,
  The Lamb for sinners slain,
Eternity is Thine abode,
  Eternal be Thy reign.

Thine eye surveys the circling years,
  All things are in Thy hand;
Thou markest the course of rolling spheres,
  They move at Thy command.

The morning stars sang out for joy,
  The orbs in concert move;
The sons of God their tongues employ
  In harmony and love.

Let all the angels worship Thee,
  Sing loud ye saints on high;
His Cross secured your victory,
  Ye heard the Bridegroom's cry.

Our sins and sorrows Thou didst bear
　In dreadful agony;
To Thee we look in earnest prayer,
　Our faith shall rest on Thee.

In death's dark vale, and gloomy shade
　Distrust and fear shall flee.
We hear Thee say "Be not afraid
　My staff thy comfort be."

In the dark grave our flesh shall rest
　Of sin and death the prey;
The gloomy grave the Victor blest
　Before us led the way.

Then in the resurrection morn
　Thou Lamb for sinners slain;
Thou who didst bear the scourge and thorn,
　We'll rise and with Thee reign.

THE CROSS ONLY.

God forbid that I should glory
   Saving only in the Cross;
Joyful sing the grand old story,
   All things else I count but dross.

Worthy is the Lamb forever
   To receive our highest praise;
Sing all heaven, with glad endeavor,
   Sing all earth in joyful lays.

With our songs we bow before Him—
   Lofty strains the angels pour—
Vie with angels and adore Him,
   Than the angels praise Him more.

Here He was a "man of sorrow,"
   Oft in anguish bowed His head.
Often prayed 'till dawning morrow
   O'er the world its glories shed.

In the garden cheerless, dreary,
　　Twice upon His bended knee,
Hear your Savior so aweary,
　　"Father take this cup from me."

His disciples fled and left Him,
　　He the wine-press trod alone,
When the sword of justice cleft Him
　　For our sins did He atone.

Now upon the cross they nail Him,
　　Whelmed in agony and blood;
Fiends and demons now assail Him
　　While forsaken of His God.

Soon the earth was rudely shaking,
　　And the sun in darkness veiled:
All the realms of nature shaking,
　　Zion's daughters loudly wailed.

On the third auspicious morning
　　Angels rolled the rock away,
Friend and foe, alike forewarning
　　Of the calm triumphal day.

From the consecrated mountain
   He ascended far on high—
Olivet, thou sacred mountain!
   He has left thee for the sky.

Passing through the shining portal,
   He resumed His royal throne;
Reign forever King immortal!
   There make all Thy glories known.

The Guest Chamber.

In a large upper room for the Master prepared
When night spread its mantle and the angels
    kept ward,
Were the flock with their Shepherd, and as Moses
    had said
Was the Paschal Lamb eaten with the unleav-
    ened bread.

No leaven of wine there, nor leaven of bread,
The "fruit of the vine" shows my blood which
    is shed;
This bread and this cup bring my passion to
    view,
And keep in remembrance what I suffer for you.

Nor Judas was there all so greedy for gold,
A thief and a devil, his Master that sold;
For Him they were waiting, the priest and the
    scribe,
Who eagerly seized the vile lucre, the bribe.

When the Shepherd was smitten the flock fled
    astray,
But soon were returning the well-beaten way;
Three days in a garden He silently lay
'Till an angel came down and the stone rolled
    away.

While Mary stood weeping with sorrow-bowed
    head,
The angel assured her He was living, the dead;
In haste she departed leaving sorrow and gloom
As her Master had left in proud triumph, the
    tomb.

Soon Peter and John came in haste to the place,
For the message of Mary had quickened their
    pace;
The tomb was deserted; the grave clothes were
    there,
Nicely folded in order, with diligent care.

From a wearisome walk two disciples returned
Rehearsing the tale, how their hearts in them
    burned,

Related in order the things that He said,
And told how they knew Him "In breaking of
  bread."

There twice in the evening His disciples consort,
And twice there He meets them in that place of
  resort;
Bequeathes them His blessing of peace and good
  will,
In words once so potent the rude tempest to
  still.

In that sanctified room when the Pentecost came,
The Spirit came down like a pure lambent
  flame;
There the baptismal waters like the Spirit were
  pour'd.
Three thousand converted and join'd to the Lord.

In a vast upper room many mansions remain,
And the song which they sing is the "Lamb
  that was slain,"
While the robes that they wear are clean linen
  and white,
No candle is needed for the Lord gives them light.

Light at Evening Time.

ZECHARIAH 14, 7.

MORNING.

Primeval man; how blest his state,
For peace and joy upon him wait;
Bland zephyrs waft a rich perfume,
All Nature smiles in primal bloom.

No discord now comes on the air,
Harmonic sounds are everywhere;
By dainty fruits the trees are fill'd,
Through all the garden Adam till'd.

No noxious weeds the earth o'er spread,
Nor noisome vapors overhead;
No beast of prey lurks to destroy;
Nor hateful reptile to annoy.

To sate his hunger man applied
To fairest fruits, on every side;
He slakes his thirst at fount or rill,
Obedient to his Maker's will.

NOON.

Misguided man! How changed his state;
More terrible impending fate;
To Eden fair he bids adieu,
Its fruitful bowers no more to view.

But doom'd to daily irksome toil,
To cultivate the sterile soil;
With throbbing brow to eat his bread;
With scanty fare his table spread.

Like beast of prey man gloats in blood,
Averse to holiness and God;
Of every vice a willing slave,
Of lust insatiate as the grave.

Earth's vast creation writhes in pain,
Vice has its many millions slain;
From earth and sea to vaulted skies
The wails of untold sorrows rise.

EVENING.

The Second Adam shall restore
What the First Adam lost before;

The wasted earth shall well repair;
And purify the baleful air.

The barren fields from long repose
Revive, and blossom as the rose;
While beasts and birds as harmless prove
As timid lamb or turtle-dove.

The lion with the lamb shall lie,
The tiger cease his frightful cry;
The timid dames dismiss their fears,
And children live a hundred years.

New heavens and earth will God create,
And man regain his primal state;
All nature swell this tuneful chime,
"It shall be light at evening-time."

THE CLEANSING FOUNTAIN.

A Fountain is open for you and for me,
Like the waves of the ocean, so boundless and free;
Like the breeze in the forest with aroma sweet,
The senses regaling with pleasure complete.

CHORUS.

O! Come to the Fountain, be cleansed from your
     stains
In the water and blood, from Immanuel's veins.

'Twas not in a garden, of green shady bowers;
Where the way-worn and weary pluck beautiful
     flowers;
Where strains of sweet music fall soft on the ear,
The spirit transporting by harmony clear.
        CHORUS: O! Come.

To a lone dreary garden see your Savior repair
On His face prostrate falling in agonized prayer;

Hear Him cry to His Father "Why forsake now
    Thy Son?
Yet O! Father not my will, but Thy will be done."
        CHORUS: O! Come.

The thorn and the purple, the nail and the spear
Close up the sad drama; the angels appear;
Death's bands cannot hold Him, the conqüering
    King;
Let earth now be joyful, and heaven loudly sing.
        CHORUS: O! Come.

Like the dew-drops descending on Hermon's fair
    Mount
Are the blessings unnumbered from this sancti-
    fied Fount;
We'll lave in its waters that cleans us from sin,
As the Syrian leper was in Jordan made clean.
        CHORUS: O! Come.

This Fountain of cleansing we hail with delight
As the lost and benighted hail the dawning of light;
Unbounded its fulness, unceasing its flow,
Assuaging our sorrows, relieving our woe.
        CHORUS: O! Come to the Fountain.

SORROW.

No other word can so express
　Man's portion here as sorrow;
Our dearest friends whom we caress
　May bid adieu to-morrow.

The broken tie to earthly bliss
　Fills full our hearts with sorrow;
We always should remember this,
　And boast not of to-morrow.

Death comes apace with shaft and bow,
　Swift flies his fatal arrow;
Unbidden tears in torrents flow
　Like waters in a furrow.

So Jesus wept while here on earth,
　Oft was o'erwhelmed in sorrow;
No time, no taste for senseless mirth,
　We should His pattern borrow.

There surely is a better land
 Beyond the reach of sorrow;
Our tears of grief shall have an end,
 We'll greet our friends to-morrow.

In that fair land of blissful rest,
 Which we may gain to-morrow;
A hand unseen supremely blest
 Shall wipe the tear of sorrow.

Thanksgiving Hymn.

Thanks to Thee Thou bounteous Giver,
　For supplies of needful food,
Flowing daily like a river,
　From the Fount of every good.

Health and friendship, precious treasure
　From our Father's bounteous hand;
Home and plenty without measure;
　Peace prevailing through the land.

Far above all price the message
　In the Gospel of Thy Son.
Most minutely page and passage
　Shows us what Thy grace has done.

"Bread of life" O! Daily give us
　"Living water" gifts of love;
Then at last do Thou receive us
　To our endless home above.

The Apostles' Creed.

PARAPHRASED.

I believe in God the Father;
  Tremblingly His name repeat;
Endless glories round Him gather—
  Bow adoring at His feet.

I believe in the Messiah
  Jesus Christ, God's equal Son;
Find in Him my chief desire,
  Trust my all in Him alone.

He who came in human nature
  To redeem from sin and death,
Once appear'd in infant stature,
  Came from heaven to earth beneath.

I believe His crucifixion
  Which He suffer'd in my stead;
I believe His resurrection,
  That He rose and left the dead.

I believe in His appearing
   Once again to judge mankind;
But my heart is sometimes fearing
   That I may be left behind.

Equal honor to the Spirit
   Cheerfully do I accord:
Far beyond angelic merit,
   Father, Spirit and the Word.

Maranatha, I receive it,
   "Come, Lord, Jesus, quickly come;"
Maranatha, I believe it,
   Come and take Thy children home,

To the Father, Son and Spirit
   Equal praise and glory be;
Laud each name, angels revere it;
   Three in one and one in three.

Definition of Patience.

BY A SCOTTISH GIRL.

"Wait a wee and dinna weary"
    Said a litte Scottish child.
Through the night, though dark and dreary,
    Through the tempest fierce and wild.

Scottish maid! Thy words of beauty
    Come to us across the sea;
Point to us the path of duty.
    Patiently we'll wait a wee.

This is what the prophet told us
    In the ages long ago:
"Lasting arms shall e'en uphold us"
    Its fulfillment God will show.

Firmly stand when foes assail us,
    Sad and dark our path may be,

Cheerful songs may there avail us
Patiently we'll wait a wee.

In the darkness daily, nightly,
Fairest visions we may see,
Beatific; shining brightly;
Patiently we'll wait a wee.

Drought, and Opportune Rain.

All Nature mourns the drought severe:
The fields and forests parched and sere.
The tunefull birds forebear to sing;
The earth withholds its offering.

The burning sun from day to day
Incessant pours its scourching ray;
No cloud umbrageous now is seen
The sun and dusty earth between.

"The lowing herds roam o'er the lea,"
Where grass abundant used to be;
The cisterns and the streams are dry;
God waits to hear His children cry!

Nor shall they cry to Him in vain;
His stores can give redundant rain;

Refreshing showers descend to bless,
And earth resumes her gorgeous dress.

'Tis the reviving of the dead.
Man's boding fears dispelled and fled.
"God in the wilderness can spread
A table" of the choicest bread.

Baptismal Waters.

"He shall sprinkle the nations," both Gentile and
    Jew;
"Clear water" is plenty in rain-drop and dew;
But the agent in cleansing is the Lamb's sprin-
    kled blood,
It makes us accepted as children of God.

Limpid water is typic and points to the blood
Which cleanses the sinner and brings him to God;
Assuages the thirst of the penitent poor
It serves a "good conscience" tho' it sprinkle or
    pour.

Oft Babel's proud monarch was "wet by the dew"
As year after year so laggardly flew;
'Till reason returned like morn after night
Or the life-bringing current after winter's long
    blight.

When Jacob left Egypt by Moses' command
The sea was a wall on the right and left hand;

Pure water came down from a cloud overhead*
Baptizing the people by Moses then led.†

On the hands of Elijah "Clean water was pour'd"
By his servant Gehazi, the scriptures record.
When from market the people went home to eat
　　bread
Their hands they baptized the scriptures have
　　said.

Six pitchers of water for occasional use
At Cana were furnished; there was never excuse
For neglectful defilement: the water was pure;
By sprinkling or pouring their cleansing was sure.

Two disciples went forth by command of their
　　Lord
A room to secure which would comfort afford;
In quest of a chamber; a good man they meet
With a pitcher of water for their hands and their
　　feet.

To the house of Cornelius Simon Peter went in,
And there preached the Gospel; salvation from
　　sin.

---

*Ps. LXXVII, 16-20.   †1 Cor. 10, 2.

None there withheld water for baptismal rite
For the hard heart was broken, and the spirit
    contrite.

In the scriptural cleansing, clean water is used
In the name of Father and Spirit diffused;
And the sweet name of Jesus is added thereto,
Only these are essential to make the rite true.

His yoke is so easy His burden so light
There need be no turning to left or to right.
In the jail at Phillippi was water to lave.
For Christian ablution what more could one crave?

A Dedicatory Hymn.

Our votive thanks to Thee we bring,
O, Lord, our Maker and our King;
Our hearts and voices here we raise
And join to celebrate Thy praise.

Long may this house be Thine abode,
An earthly palace for our God;
The three in one, and one in three,
Fill every heart with ecstacy.

Here prayer and praise be our employ,
While we express our holy joy;
Abundant peace may we possess
From Thee, O Lord, our righteousness.

The Gospel of good will to men,
Of Him who once for us was slain,
Be spoken in sincerity;
Our constant theme it e'er shall be.

With joy, the summons we'll obey
That calls us here, from earth away;
No other place can well compare
With this our Father's house of prayer.

All glory to the living God;
The highest heav'n is His abode;
Our highest honors here we bring
And sound the praises of our King.

PURE WATER.

It glistens in the morning dew,
　　Descends in fruitful showers;
It murmurs in the merry brook,
　　And cheers the vocal bowers.

Gives beauty to the rainbow tint
　　And beauty to the flower;
Gives vigor to the lab'ring swain
　　And nerves his arm with power.

'Tis chosen for baptismal rite,
　　The sacrament divine;
A fitting emblem 'tis, through which
　　The cleansing graces shine.

It percolates the teeming earth,
　　It permeates the air;
It pulsates in our num'rous veins
　　Is present every everywhere.

It rushes through the shady dell,
　It leaps adown the mountain ;
It sparkles in the crystal well,
　And gushes from the fountain.

Oft as we quaff the healthful draught
　This boon benignly given,
We'll pray that we may freely share
　The antitype in heaven.

God our Refuge.

PSALM 46.

The Lord is our refuge, our fortress and tower
　When troubles assail us then God is our shield.
We'll trust His protection when angry clouds lower
　Tho' earth rudely tremble, our faith shall not
　　. yield.

When loud howls the tempest in God we'll confide,
　The winds and the billows obey His behest;
Through storm and o'er billow in safety we'll ride
　Obeying His fiat, the billows shall rest.

Here flow crystal waters; perennial waters,
　To gladden fair Zion, the city of God.
O! Come to the waters, ye famishing daughters
　For here is provided a peaceful abode.

Munitions of warfare, the spear and the arrow
　Are futile devices when God is shield;
Our foes shall inherit confusion and sorrow
　While He to His children His aid shall afford.

UNIVERSAL PRAISE.

Let all the people praise the Lord.
Join heart and voice in one accord.
In lofty strains ye angels bring
Due tribute to your heavenly King.

We praise Thee for Thy love to man;
Through heaven the joyful tidings ran;
And angels brought the news to earth,
Glad tidings of the Savior's birth.

His love to man we celebrate,
Who was rejected by the great;
All other joys we count but dross,
And glory only in the Cross.

We praise Thee for Thy Spirit given
To lead our wayward feet to heaven;
The heart of stone to take away
And lead us in the better way.

We praise Thee for Thy day of rest
Most precious, most divinely blest;
We praise Thee for Thy Book divine,
In which such grace and glory shine.

We praise Thee for the gift of song;
Thy love inspiring heart and tongue.
No such delight can earth afford.
Let all the people praise the Lord.

THE POISON WEED.

Of all the vile and noxious weeds
  By which the earth is cursed
For sinful man's depravity,
  Tobacco is the worst.

Man's primal work it was
  To keep the garden fair:
The orange and the lemon bloomed,
  The rose perfumed the air.

"Prohibit" was engraved upon
  One solitary tree;
"Taste not nor touch forbidden fruit"
  All other fruit was free.

Infracted was the stern command:
  The woman made for man,
Was lured, deceived, ensnared in sin:
  Sorrow and death began.

In vengeful wrath Jehovah said
  The thistle and the thorn,
The fruitful earth shall soon o'erspread
  And choke the growing corn.—

Jannes and Jambus once withstood
  Two holy men of God;
And seeming miracles they wrought
  Like those by Aaron's rod.

So Satan thought within himself
  To equal or exceed;
And instantly by magic skill
  Produced a poison weed.

It penetrates the food we eat,
  It permeates the air;
Is forced into reluctant lungs,
  Like pestilential air.—

'Tis sending up a baleful smoke
  Like Tartarus below;
It binds its victims to a yoke
  Of misery and woe.—

The glory of Mount Lebanon
  The fir-tree dressed in green,
Shall well adorn the verdant earth
  Where briars and thorns have been.

The mountain and the plains shall sing;
  The islands of the sea;
"No poison weed, no poison drink,
  It is earth's jubilee."

LET ME DIE SOBER.

O let me die sober when summoned away,
My life gently fading like evening's last ray;
O let me die sober, for who could desire
Expiring in darkness—as meteors expire?

O let me die sober, as martyrs have died,
In righteousness clad, like the robes of a bride;
In peace with my conscience, in peace with man-
     kind,
The earth with its trifles and pomps left behind,

The waves in commotion leap up in delight,
Exulting from joy, kiss the ocean-washed height.
Exempted from bondage, in triumph I'll sing
Of unsullied pleasures, no wine-cup can bring.

Vile poisonous nostrums have tainted the air,
Humanity pleading, cries "doctor! borbear,"
With vision unclouded while struggling with
     death
I'll show to the skeptic the triumph of faith.

See priest at the altar misguided through wine
Abihu and Nadab, through fruit of the vine;
Then let me die sober when passing away
And quaff limpid waters in lands far away.

MALUM PERSE.

——◆——

"With the point of a diamond" as all men may see
Are written strange letters; they are m-a-l-u-m-
  p-e-r-s-e;
A demon is lurking in wine-cup and bowl,
It poisons the body, it fetters the soul.

The fang of the serpent, the adder's fell sting
To man, when in sorrow, no solace can bring;
Their badge and their venom time can never set free;
Forever remaineth their m-a-l-u-m-p-e-r-s-e.

Mystic letters were written in Babel of old
Near the vessels of silver, and goblets of gold;
M-e-n-e-t-e-k-e-l-u-p-h-a-r-s-i-n, for Belshazzar to see:
The wine in those vessels, was m-a-l-u-m-p-e-r-s-e.

Away with the wine-cup; I spurn its control,
It poisons the body, it fetters the soul;
From the fetters it forges thank God I am free.
Indelibly written is m-a-l-u-m-p-e-r-s-e.

O Tempore! O Mores!

O Tempore! O Mores! I am led to exclaim
When I think of my country's dishonor and
    shame.
Three pence for each pound was the tax on the tea
Which our puritan fathers cast into the sea.

A tax and a burden more galling has come
Enshrouding our nation in sorrow and gloom;
While those who should aid us refuse us their aid
Their chief occupation political trade!

The oak in the forest with branches spread wide
Through the centuries past has the tempest defied.
The oak in the forest betokens decay,
As branch after branch to the ground falls away.

Would you seek for the reason? the reason we see,
A worm is at work in the trunk of the tree;
And slowly but surely is eating its way
Every inch that is eaten, but hastens decay.

A beautiful tree in our land has long stood,
Its graceful proportions and fruit very good;
Enriched by the blood of our sires gone before
Sends its umbrageous shadow to the most distant
　　shore.

Our Puritan fathers cross a turbulent sea,
On the soil of New England plant this beautiful tree;
Soon the birds of ill omen flap their wings as
　　they come
With the vessel that brings the first cargo of rum.

" *Sic semper tyrannis* " inscribed let it be
Through the land cis-Atlantic; the land of the free;
We spurn the dominion of lager and rum;
Let law give protection to loved ones and home.

Shall we tax or give licence? both mean the same
　　thing
A few paltry dollars paltry revenue bring;
Let the ballots of freemen their purpose fulfill
And hasten the death of the worm of the still.

THE EXODUS.

———◆———

Can the spots of the leopard of various hue
Be changed by volition, his nature be new?
Can the Ethiop's dermis so somber and tan
Become at his bidding just like the white man?

Can prickling brambles grapes ever afford
With "wine in the cluster" each cell with it
        stored?
Can the fig from the thistle evolve for our use?
Can the alkaline fountains sweet water produce?

It never can be, the thing is absurd;
No such freak of nature has ever occurred;
Since "like begets like" it is dame natures rule,
Who thinks otherwise is next to a fool.

"God mend me." This sentence the poet often used
Whenever he blundered, from being confused.
The page in his presence scanned the ill-shapen man
And quickly responded as only boys can.

· "'Twould better befit him to make something new,
Than taxing his patience to remodel you."
The thought is a good one ; God works in this way
The old in removing which threatens decay.

The great Martin Luther, heroic and true
"A wise master builder" from the base builded new ;
On a rocky foundation the building must stand,
'Till the waves shall recede from the surf-beaten
strand.

The greatest Reformer the world ever knew,
Of Him it is written "I make everything new."
With Him for our Leader, His word for our guide
Our foes shall surrender whatever betide.

Temperance Revival.

Say what means this great commotion
  Through the borders of the land,
Like the billows of the ocean,
  Rushing proudly on the strand;
  Rising grandly; dashing proudly on the strand.

Why this rising through the nation
  Like the swelling of the sea?
'Tis the omen of salvation;
  Boding certain victory.
  Joyful token, harbinger of victory.

Stormy winds and ocean rolling
  Have a purpose to fulfill.
One there is, all things controlling,
  They obey His sovereign will,
  Blowing, flowing, they obey His sovereign will.

Like a fragile vessel, broken
  Was the power of Greece and Rome;
When the Lord the word had spoken

Babel met a righteous doom.
Long since buried in a long forgotten tomb.

Egypt saw Jehovah's token
    When He came His own to save;
Saw her frightened legions broken,
    Saw them sink beneath the wave.
    O'er those legions saw the angry waters rave.

God of nations! if Thou guide us,
    And we follow Thy command,
Righteous laws if Thou provide us,
    Truth and right pervade the land,
    We securely on a firm foundation stand.

The Song of Bacchus.

Most jubilant is Bacchus,
  And this is what he sings;
Our friends will not forsake us,
  My army has two wings.

Two pillars has my temple,
  It could not stand alone;
And their support so ample
  Shall well sustain my throne.

Now when the pillars tremble
  Shout "Great is Diana"
Let all my friends assemble
  And form one grand array.

In halls of legislation
  I'm speaker by consent,
'Tis not by usurpation
  My friends all seem content.

For preaching and for praying
  I do not care one fig.

While they their prayers are saying
  I'll laugh and dance a jig.

But now the truth I'm speaking
  One thing my courage shocks
And makes me feel like sneaking
  I dread the *ballot-box*.

I have no lack of money
  Unbounded wealth is mine.
To some it may seem funny,
  I make the whisky wine.

Some preachers give no trouble
  Their views are very calm,
Transparent as a bubble;
  They cause me no alarm.

The Bible through their teaching,
  Is handmaid to my cause;
Their practice and their preaching
  Elicit my applause.

Moreover, through their teaching
  The Bible justifies
The use of wine; (by stretching)
  Good men must it despise.

Temperance Rally.

We are coming, we are coming,
A million freemen strong,
And since our hearts are merry
We will sing a merry song.

Tho' little our beginning,
So everything must be,
The little grain of mustard
Has now become a tree.

A little ball was rolling
Along the melting snow,
See how the rolling snow-balls
To huge proportions grow.

A pebble in the ocean
May yet an island be,
And just a little acorn
Become the monarch tree.

Throw a pebble in the ocean
　　It will there create commotion,
Nor shall die away the motion
　　'Til it reach the distant shore.

We have vowed entire devotion
　　And will keep the wave in motion,
'Til it reach across the ocean,
　　And our sacred rights restore.

The foe begins to tremble,
　　And to shake his hoary locks;
He is filled with consternation,
　　Just to see the ballot-box.

He constantly is prating
　　Of liberty his own,
But will rob you of your money
　　As a mastiff picks a bone.

We are done with our petitions—
　　Time and paper thrown away,
You have mocked the weeping women
　　'Til their locks are turned to gray.

But a righteous retribution
  Is now waiting at your door,
And a storm of indignation
  Shall like a torrent pour.

We will flaunt the temp'rance banner
  On each hill-top and savanna,
Be the sacred word hossanna,
  On the breezes sent afar.

With the God of hosts before us
  We will swell the chorus,
'Til the heavens o'er us
  Shall resound the loud huzza.

MT. OLIVET.

Adjacent to Salem stands Mt. Olivet,
Its records of sorrow I sing in regret;
The valley of Cedron lies midway between,
Oft crossing that valley our Savior was seen.

There Martha and Mary, and Lazarus too
Of pious deportment; with Zion in view;
There diligence Martha encumbered by care
A coat without seam, did so deftly prepare.

At the table of Simon where Jesus was guest
Bore the part of a servant, by Simon's request;
Nor irksome the service: but scrupulous care
Displayed at the table: opportunity rare.

There penitent Mary, whose profusion of tears
Betokened her grief, for her guilt of past years,
Betokened her love, for he freely forgave
And wakened her brother from death and the grave.

Lazarus there, in the sepulcher slept,
Four days was he sleeping, and there "Jesus wept,"
But woke at the call of the Master who said
"Come forth thou that sleepest, arise from the
dead."—

At the close of each day he sought for repose
Away from the City, secure from his foes;
Not once in the City did he tarry all night
But traversed the valley, to Olivet's hight.

Oft chilled by the night-winds and wet by the dew
Disciple and Master held sad interview—
The end is approaching with little delay
From the flock must the shepherd be taken away.

At midnight together they silently go,
Or words if then spoken were trembling and low.
The last word was uttered in blessing bestowed,
The master ascended; his chariot a cloud.

JUDGMENT HYMN.

Hear the trump of Gabriel sounding
  Pealing through the vaulted skies,
Far and wide through earth resounding,
  Lo! The sleeping dead arise,
In amazement, in amazement,
  See the sleeping dead arise.

Now He comes to earth returning
  His rewards with Him to bring,
While the earth is rent and burning,
  Saints rejoice. He comes. Your King.
Now returning, now returning;
  Saints rejoice. He comes. Your King.

Saints and angels are attending,
  Now they come in bright array,
Down to earth their pinions bending,
  Long has seemed my Lord's delay
Bow before him, bow before him,
  Let there be no more delay.

Now the guilty ones assemble,
  Blank despair fills every heart,
Speechless now; they pale and tremble
  When they hear their doom "Depart."
Loud their wailing, loud their wailing
  At the stern command "Depart."

www.ingramcontent.com/pod-product-compliance
Lightning Source LLC
Chambersburg PA
CBHW020405030726
47496CB00007B/2309